Lila on the Landing

LILA
on the Landing

by Sue Alexander

drawings by Ellen Eagle

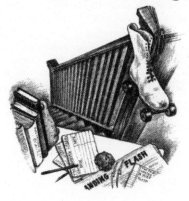

CLARION BOOKS
NEW YORK

Clarion Books
a Houghton Mifflin Company imprint
215 Park Avenue South, New York, NY 10003
Text copyright © 1987 by Sue Alexander
Illustrations copyright © 1987 by Ellen Eagle

Library of Congress Cataloging-in-Publication Data
Alexander, Sue, 1933–
Lila on the landing.
Summary: Lila, always the last to be chosen for
games by the other children, earns their interest
and acceptance by creating her own imaginative
activities on the landing of her apartment house.
[1. Imagination—Fiction. 2. Play—Fiction.
3. Individuality—Fiction. 4. Apartment houses—
Fiction] I. Eagle, Ellen, ill. II. Title.
PZ7.A3784Li 1987 [Fic] 87-301
ISBN 0-89919-340-4 PA ISBN 0-395-52597-7

FFG 10 9 8 7 6 5 4 3 2 1

To my aunt,
Dorothy Rosenberg,
with much love

chapter

· 1 ·

Something was missing.

I looked around the landing trying to figure out what it was. It wasn't anything big, I knew that. All the big things were there.

My table was angled out from the corner, and there was enough room for me to get behind it and sit down in the folding chair. My books — between the frog bookends — covered one whole side of the table. They looked nice, I thought. The pickle jar of pencils and the slips of paper I'd cut were placed neatly in back of the books. So was the shoe box that I'd marked Books Checked Out in red crayon.

It wasn't anything to wear, either. I'd put on the kind of clothes that Mrs. Markey at the library usually wore. A skirt and blouse. And sandals. Mrs. Markey wore stockings too, but since I didn't have those, I'd put on my brown tights.

"Well, Ms. Rocklin, I see we have another arrangement on the landing today," boomed a voice over my shoulder.

I jumped. I hadn't heard Mr. Zeller coming down the stairs from the third floor.

"Last week's sailing ship sailed away, eh, Lila?" Mr. Zeller's smile always lit his eyes as well as his face.

"I'm on dry land this week," I said, smiling back at him.

He chuckled as he made the turn on the landing and went on down the stairs.

All the people who lived in the building's five other apartments were used to my playing on the landing. And none of them minded. Not even Mrs. Sweeney, our landlady. Which wasn't too surprising. Mrs. Sweeney likes me a lot.

I looked back at the table. And saw what was missing. "Signs! There are always signs in a library!"

I ran down the carpeted stairs to our apartment. Mama looked up from the book she was reading as I opened the door.

"I need my pad of construction paper," I said. "Do you know where it is?"

Mama nodded. "Right where you left it this morning. Over there, on the table near the sofa." She smiled and went back to her book.

As I picked up the pad of paper, I glanced out of the living room window. Alan, Amy, and Jon were on

the sidewalk in front of the apartment building next door. They had their roller skates on.

From the look on Jon's face I could tell that Alan was being bossy again. Alan seems to think that just because he's bigger than everyone else, and half-a-year older, he has the right to be boss. And most of the time we let him. I'm not sure why. Maybe it's because it's easier than arguing with him. I don't know how Amy or Jon feel, but arguing makes me shake inside. Besides, I don't really care who decides what we play.

But Alan decides *who* plays too. And that's the part I don't like. Especially since, lately, it's meant that I've been the one who didn't get to.

Like yesterday afternoon.

When I'd gone outside after school, the three of them had been playing catch.

"Throw me the ball next, Amy," I'd said. "I'll be the fourth corner."

"No," Alan had said. "You can't play. You always drop the ball."

Amy had hesitated, but then she'd thrown the ball to Jon. And he had thrown it to Alan.

I'd bitten my lip to keep it from quivering. Alan had made it sound as if I went around dropping balls on purpose! And I didn't. Not ever. "It doesn't matter," I'd said, trying to act as if I didn't care. "I have to go inside in a minute anyway." And after I'd watched them throw the ball to each other one more time, that's what I'd done.

It wasn't fair. I couldn't help it if I was clumsy. Last year it hadn't mattered; everyone else had been clumsy too. But this year it was different. I was the only one.

Mama had tried to make me feel better. "You'll grow out of it, honey," she'd said. "You'll see. By the time you're nine, you'll have forgotten that you were ever clumsy, and so will everyone else."

I hoped she was right. But even if she was, it didn't really help. I wouldn't be nine for seven more months. And I wanted to play with Amy, Alan, and Jon *now*.

I sighed and turned away from the window. Tucking the pad of construction paper under my arm, I went out of our apartment and started up the stairs to the landing. Then I stopped. Maybe today . . .

chapter
·2·

"**D**on't skate in the street."

I knew Mama would say that. She said it every time I took my skates out of the front closet.

"I won't," I promised.

Mama's head was bent over her book again; I don't think she heard me. It didn't really matter — we both had said the same things at least twenty times already this year.

By the time I got outside, Amy, Alan, and Jon were lined up for a race.

"Wait for me!" I hurried across the small patch of grass that led from our apartment building to Amy's and sat down on her stoop to put on my skates.

"You can't be in the race, Lila," Alan said. "You always fall down."

I felt myself flush. It was true. I did fall down a lot. But still . . .

"I can race if I want to," I muttered stubbornly.

"On your mark! Get set! GO!" Jon yelled.

And they were off before I could get to the starting line. They were skating so fast that the back of Amy's dress went up like a balloon. I wasn't sure I could catch up. But I was going to try.

"I won't fall. I won't fall. I won't fall," I told myself in time to the click-clack of my skates on the sidewalk. I skated past the wide yellow brick building, then the narrow brown one. "I won't . . ."

I fell.

My knee stung and there was a tear in my tights. By the time I'd put spit on the scrape, the race was over and Alan, Amy, and Jon were skating back toward me.

"Jon won," Amy told me as we all skated along the sidewalk to her apartment building.

Alan turned his head toward us and scowled. "Not by very much."

That was another thing about Alan. He didn't like to lose. At anything.

"That was fun," Jon said. "Let's have another race."

"No," Alan said, sitting down on the stoop and taking off his skates. "We'll do something else."

"Like what?" Amy wanted to know.

Alan shrugged. "Oh, I don't care. Since Jon won the race, he can think of something."

But Jon couldn't think of anything.

Maybe, I thought, they'd like to go up to my landing.

We could all play library together. "I know something to do," I said, taking off my skates and putting my sandals back on.

"What?" asked Jon.

Before I could answer, Alan said, "Amy, didn't you just get a new jump rope?"

Amy nodded. "It's a real long one."

"Go get it," Alan ordered.

Amy ran inside.

That was strange. Alan had never wanted to jump rope before. What made him want to now? It was almost — almost as if he were trying to keep me from telling my idea. But why would he want to do that? I couldn't think of any reason.

Just then Amy came back outside with her jump rope.

"You take this end," she instructed, handing Alan one of the blue handles. "Jon, you take the other. We can take turns jumping. I'll be first."

That made sense. It was her jump rope. "I'll be next," I said.

"No." Alan shook his head. "You don't get a turn."

"That's not fair, Alan," Jon protested.

"Yes, it is too," Alan insisted. "Lila would just get her feet tangled in the rope and trip. Then the game would be ruined for the rest of us."

Jon didn't argue. Neither did Amy. They didn't look at me either.

There was a smirk on Alan's face as he turned toward me. "We'll jump," he said. "You watch."

I could feel tears burning my eyes. I blinked hard to keep them from falling.

"No," I said. "I won't. I have something else I can do. Something much better than jumping rope." And I picked up my skates and went back across the small patch of grass to my apartment building.

chapter
·3·

I couldn't see.

The tears I hadn't let fall were blurring my eyes. I brushed them away and ran up the stairs to the landing.

"I don't care that he won't let me play with them — I don't!" Saying it out loud didn't make it true, but it helped. So did just sitting in my chair on the landing.

I don't know what there is about the landing that makes me feel good inside, but it does. It isn't just that it's a quiet place, or that I like the wallpaper with red roses on it. It's something else.

Maybe it's that it can be any place that I want it to be. Once it had been the hut that Heidi and her grandfather lived in (I'd worn my peasant blouse that has puffed sleeves). Another time it had been Rapunzel's tower (Mama had let me borrow her green robe with gold trimming). And then Aladdin's cave (I'd used a purple bath towel to make a turban). It had been a restaurant, a television studio, and — last week — a ship going across the ocean. I'd been a terrific ship's captain — even if Daddy's old Navy cap didn't fit exactly.

Today it was a library. As I sat there, all the plans I'd made for playing library rushed back into my head. First I was going to be somebody who came into the library to check out books. I'd have to fill out one of the slips for every book I checked out. Then I was going to be the librarian and tell stories. Maybe I'd have a crafts time too — bookmarks would be fun to make.

"I *do* have something better to do." It was true, but still . . .

I sighed and reached for one of the slips of paper. I'd check out a book. Maybe by the time I was finished reading it, I *really* wouldn't care that I was playing by myself instead of with Amy, Alan, and Jon.

The landing window was open, and I heard Amy laughing at something. I winced and made myself concentrate on what I was doing. When I finished filling out the slip, I put it in the slot on the lid of the shoe box. Then I settled back in my chair and opened the book I'd taken from between the bookends.

That's when I heard Alan yell.

"There has to be something better to do than jumping rope!"

I wondered what had happened. Putting my book down, I went over to the window and looked out.

The jump rope lay on the ground, and Alan and Amy were standing over it, glaring at each other. Jon was standing on the grass, shuffling his feet nervously. Then he shrugged and walked away.

A minute later I heard the downstairs door creak open. By the time I turned around, Jon was coming up the stairs.

"I saw you in the window," he said. "What are you doing up here?" He looked over at the table, and his eyes opened wide. "It looks like a *library*!"

The surprise in his voice made me giggle. "It *is* a library," I said. "Would you like to check out a book?"

Jon didn't answer. He just stood there, looking from me to the books and back again. Then he nodded. "I guess so. It's better than listening to Alan and Amy argue about what to do." And he smiled.

I went back to my chair. "Pick out the book you want to read," I said in my best librarian voice. "There are all kinds of books to choose from."

Jon came up to the table. "Is there one that tells about bugs?" he asked. "I'm starting a bug collection. So far I have two flies, some ants, and a spider."

I couldn't help shuddering. I don't like spiders at all.

Jon grinned. "Don't worry," he said reassuringly. "They're all dead. My mother won't let me keep live ones in the house." He looked down at the books for a moment and then pulled a green one from between the

bookends. *"Your Backyard World,"* he read aloud. "This one ought to have bugs in it."

"It does," I said. "But before you read it, you'll need to check it out." I handed him one of the slips of paper.

He sat down on the stairs to look at it.

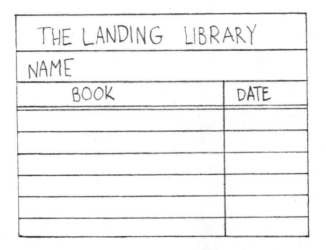

Just then Amy's voice floated up from outside. "Hurry up, Alan!"

Jon looked up.

He's going to tell me that he's changed his mind about playing library and go back outside, I thought. I took a deep breath and waited.

But all he said was, "I don't have a pencil."
I let out my breath.
And gave him a pencil from the pickle jar.

chapter

·4·

J on let out a low whistle.

"This is a neat book," he said. "It's got lots of pictures of bugs."

I remembered those pictures. They were the reason I'd only read that book once.

"You have a bunch of neat books," Jon said, looking over at the table. "Maybe I'll check out another one when I'm finished with this one."

"You could," I agreed. "Or you could listen to a story. My library is going to have a story time."

"Story time! Who's going to tell stories?"

"The librarian, of course. Me."

"What story are you going to tell?" Jon asked.

" 'The Mouse and the Dragon.' "

Jon shook his head. "I never heard of that one."

"No, you never did," I said. "You couldn't have."

He looked puzzled. "Why not?"

"Because I made it up."

"*You* made it up?" Jon stared at me as if he'd never seen me before. "That's neat!"

It made me feel good to know that he thought I'd done something special — even though I hadn't. Making up stories was something that I did all the time. I'd made this one up last night before I fell asleep. It was what had given me the idea to play library on the landing.

"Tell your story now," Jon said. "I'll finish the book later." He closed the book, put it down on the stair beside him, and looked at me expectantly.

"All right." I boosted myself up on the table.

Jon looked at me curiously.

"Mrs. Markey at the library always sits on the table when she tells stories," I explained.

With a quick nod of understanding, Jon settled back against the stairs.

"Once upon a time," I began, "there was a mouse who was very brave."

Just then the downstairs door opened.

"Lila? Jon? Are you up there?" Alan's voice floated up the stairwell.

My stomach did a flip-flop. Did Alan want us to come back outside? I didn't want to go. Alan would probably just be mean to me again. Maybe if I didn't answer, he'd go away. But if I didn't answer, Jon would. So — I might as well. "Yes," I called down, "we're here."

Alan came up the stairs. Amy was right behind him.

"Amy said this was where you went," Alan said, talking directly to Jon. "What are you doing up here?"

"I'm telling a story," I said. "We're playing library and it's story time."

"Library! Story time! That's dumb!"

I winced. "No, it's *not*," I said.

The table might just as well have spoken, for all the attention Alan paid.

"Come on, Jon, let's go *do* something."

I felt my stomach tighten. It doesn't matter, I told myself. I can still play library. I don't need Jon. I don't need anyone. *It doesn't matter.*

Jon shook his head. "Listening to a story *is* doing something."

"Not to me, it's not," Alan snapped.

Jon shrugged.

Angry red blotches broke out on Alan's face. He turned and glared at me.

Why was he angry with *me* because Jon decided to stay on the landing? It didn't make any sense.

"Come on, Amy, let's go."

Amy started down the stairs after Alan. Then she stopped and came back up to the landing. "What story are you telling?"

" 'The Mouse and the Dragon.' "

She frowned. "I don't know that story."

"That's because Lila made it up," Jon said importantly.

"Oh!" Amy looked at me in surprise.

"Amy! Come on!" Alan's voice echoed up the stairwell.

Amy hesitated. Then, with a sigh, she turned and went slowly down the stairs.

I stared after her. She would have liked to hear my story, I was sure of it. Then why hadn't she stayed? Just because Alan didn't want her to? For that matter, what was Alan so angry about? Because playing library hadn't been his idea? No. It was something else. But exactly what, I didn't know.

Well, I wasn't going to worry about it. At least not now. I had a story to tell — and someone who wanted to hear it. I smiled at Jon and began again.

"Once upon a time . . ."

chapter
·5·

$\mathbf{M}$y knee hit the table leg.

I yelled — and Mrs. Sweeney's door opened. I'm not as brave as the mouse in the story I told yesterday. Sometimes, when I get hurt, everybody within hearing distance knows it.

"Everything's all right, Mrs. Sweeney," I called up to the third floor. Her door closed.

That's the thing about scrapes; they feel worse the day after you get them. Well, I wouldn't get another one today. I wasn't going to try to skate. I wasn't even going to go outside. I'd thought of something else to do.

Shifting in my chair, I smoothed out the pad of lined paper on the table in front of me and read what I'd written.

I knew what was going to happen in the play. I'd thought it all out on my way home from school and while I was changing into my playwriting blue pants and sweater. Now I had to decide what each of my play

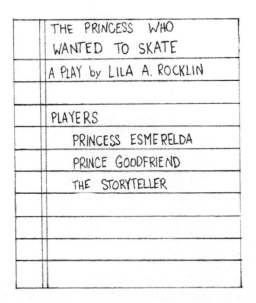

THE PRINCESS WHO
WANTED TO SKATE

A PLAY by LILA A. ROCKLIN

PLAYERS
   PRINCESS ESMERELDA
   PRINCE GOODFRIEND
   THE STORYTELLER

people would say. The storyteller (there was another word for that, but I didn't know it) would talk first, to tell where and when everything was happening. I closed my eyes and tried to see it all in my head.

"Lila, are you asleep?"

Jon's voice startled me. I'd been thinking so hard that I hadn't heard the downstairs door open. I opened my eyes.

Amy was there too. She had a worried look on her face.

"No, I'm not asleep," I said. "I was thinking."

"Were you thinking about what story to tell for today's library story time?" Amy asked, smiling her relief.

I shook my head. "The landing isn't a library today."

"Oh." Amy's smile faded. "It looked like fun," she said wistfully.

"It was," Jon said. He looked disappointed too.

I just sat there, staring at them. I'd known why Jon had come up to the landing yesterday, but I never thought that he'd come back. Or that Amy would come with him.

"I was hoping you'd tell another story about that mouse," Jon said. "It was neat how he scared the dragon."

Amy sighed. "I wanted to hear your story yesterday," she said, "but I'd promised Alan that I would play with him." Then she added, "I didn't walk home with him today."

For a minute I considered forgetting about my play and telling a story instead. I could do it — but I really didn't want to.

"If the landing isn't a library, what is it?" A puzzled frown had settled on Jon's face.

"It's a stage for a play," I said. "I'm writing the play now. That's what I was thinking about."

"A play!" Amy's mouth and eyes both opened wide.

Jon leaned over and looked at what I'd written. " 'The

Princess Who Wanted to Skate,' " he read aloud.

"Oh! I love princesses!" A big smile lit Amy's face. "Does your princess do something important?"

I didn't know how to answer that. What the people in my plays did was important to *me*. Lots of times I made up a story or a play because I wanted to change something that really happened into what I *wanted* to happen. Like this play. Princess Esmerelda was going to get to be the best skater in the whole world.

"Well . . ." I began slowly.

Jon wasn't interested in my answer. There was something else he wanted to know. "After you write the play, who's going to act it out?"

"I am."

"All by *yourself*?" Amy asked.

Her question startled me. I had always acted out my plays by myself. I started to tell Amy that — then I stopped. There had been something in her voice. . . .

Suddenly I knew what it was. Amy wanted to be in my play! I looked over at Jon. Did he want to be in it too?

The idea of anyone besides me acting out one of my plays made a shiver go up my back. I stared down at the words I'd written. Nobody but me had ever even *read* one of my plays. They had always been something I'd done just for myself.

Did I want anyone else to be in the play with me?

chapter
·6·

"What are you thinking?"

I could hear the hope in Amy's voice. Maybe it *would* be fun to act out my play with somebody else. I'd try it. "I'm thinking that you both can be in the play with me if you want to," I said.

Amy nodded happily. "I want to," she said.

"Who would I be?" Jon asked.

"The prince."

Jon looked suddenly uneasy. "Is it the kind of play where the prince has to kiss the princess? Because if it is, I don't want to be in it."

Amy and I both laughed.

"No," I told Jon, "the prince just looks happy at the end."

Relief spread over Jon's face. "I can do that," he said.

Amy sat down on the stairs. "Hurry up and finish writing the play, Lila."

Pulling a piece of string out of his jeans pocket, Jon

sat down on the stairs next to Amy and made a cat's cradle on his fingers.

I watched him for a minute, then I bent my head over the pad of paper and began to write.

"Who talks first, Lila?" Amy asked.

"The storyteller," I answered without looking up.

"What does the storyteller say?"

"Lila can't write the play if you keep talking, Amy," Jon complained.

I glanced up and saw Amy stick out her tongue at Jon. Then she grinned. "Show me how to make a cat's cradle and I won't talk."

I watched Jon thread the string through Amy's fingers. Then I went back to my play. The words my play people would say began to come quickly to mind, and I wrote as fast as I could. Five pieces of paper later, I was finished. I sighed and leaned back in my chair.

"Is the play ready now?" Amy asked eagerly.

I nodded, suddenly too tired to talk.

Jon took the pages of the play from me and, leaning back against the stairs, read them out loud. It felt strange hearing my words coming out of somebody else's mouth. My heart began to beat very fast, and the back of my neck got hot. I squirmed in my chair and stared at a rose on the wallpaper.

"It's a neat play, Lila!"

Jon's words made me feel good.

Amy bounced on the stair excitedly. "It's going to be fun to do!"

My tired feeling went away. It *was* going to be fun.

"I want to be the princess," Amy said, smoothing out the skirt of her dress.

That was not what I'd had in mind. I'd written that part for me. "No," I said. "I'm going to."

"It's Lila's play," Jon said. "She *should* be the princess."

Amy's lower lip jutted out.

Maybe my saying she could be in my play hadn't been a good idea after all. Then I thought of a way to make it all right. "We can both be the princess," I said. "We'll put on the play twice. I'll be the princess first, then you will."

"That's fair," Jon said quickly.

Amy smoothed out her skirt again. "All right," she agreed reluctantly. "I'll be the storyteller this time." She took the play from Jon and went to the center of the landing. First she bowed. Then, in the same singsong voice that she read poems out loud in school, she began.

"Over the hills and far away, there was a kingdom called . . ."

The downstairs door opened, and Alan's voice echoed up the stairwell. "Lila? Are Amy and Jon up there?"

"Oh good! He can be the audience!" Amy went to the

top of the stairs. "We're here, Alan," she called down. "Come on up!"

I had a sinking feeling in my stomach.

"No! You come down!"

"Not now, Alan." Jon leaned over the banister. "We're busy."

Alan ran up the stairs. "Busy doing what?" he demanded.

"We're putting on a play," Amy said excitedly. "It's about a princess. Lila wrote it."

Alan flushed angrily. "A play about a princess," he mocked. "Stu-pid!" He scowled at me.

"Princesses aren't stupid!" Amy protested.

"Oh, who cares!" Alan said. "It doesn't matter." He stopped and looked around to make sure we were all listening. "I have a new bike!"

"New bike!" Jon jumped up. "What kind is it? When did you get it?"

"My dad brought it home this afternoon," Alan said. "I was waiting for you to come outside so I could show it to you." He scowled at me again.

"Will you let us ride it?" Amy asked.

"Sure," Alan said grandly. "Come on." He started down the stairs.

Jon hurried after him.

"Let's go, Lila." Amy put the play on the table.

Before I could get up from my chair, Alan came back up the stairs. "Not Lila," he said. "She can't have a ride. She'd just fall and bang up my new bike."

I bit my lip and looked toward the window.

"Alan, that's not . . ." Amy's voice trailed off, and she sighed. Then I heard her start down the stairs.

Out of the corner of my eye I saw a smile on Alan's face as he turned to follow her. It wasn't a nice smile.

The downstairs door slammed shut. They were gone.

I was by myself — again.

chapter
· 7 ·

I shivered.

My arm bumped the table, and the pages of the play fell on the floor. I stared down at them. It would have been fun to act it out with Amy and Jon. If only Alan hadn't come up to the landing!

But — he had. There wasn't anything I could do about that. But there was something I could do about my play. Put it on anyway. The way I'd planned to in the beginning. By myself.

I picked up the play and started to say Princess Esmerelda's first line. "I want so much to . . ." My voice sounded as if I'd dragged it over pebbles. I swallowed — and tasted salt.

There wasn't any point in going on. I didn't feel like a princess. I didn't even feel like putting on my play. The fun had gone out of it.

I put the play on the table and went downstairs.

"I'm in here, honey!" Mama's voice came from the kitchen.

Sheets of press-on letters and pieces of cardboard were spread all over the kitchen table. Mama was staring at them, worry wrinkles lining her forehead. "I told Mrs. Strand that these letters were too big," she complained.

Mama was doing her homework. At least, that's what I called the projects that the teachers at my school gave the parent helpers to do.

I took a glass from the cupboard next to the sink and turned on the tap. Maybe a drink of water would wash away the salty tightness in my throat.

Mama looked up and smiled. "Halloween flash cards for the first grade," she explained.

My throat felt too tight to talk. I nodded.

Mama's smile faded. "What's the matter, honey?" she asked gently.

When I didn't answer, she said, "I heard the downstairs door close. I thought you all had left the building."

"*They* left." The words burst out. I swallowed and tasted salt again. "Alan came up. He got a new bike and . . ."

I couldn't go on. I turned and ran down the hall to my bedroom. The bed swayed as I flopped down on it and buried my face in the pillow.

How could I explain why Alan was so mean to me when I didn't understand it myself? I hadn't done anything to him. At least nothing that I could think of. Besides, it wasn't Alan's being mean that hurt. It was Amy and Jon. They didn't *have* to go with Alan. They wanted to.

"I should never have said they could be in my play in the first place," I muttered into my pillow.

Well, I wouldn't make that mistake again. Until Jon came up to the landing, the games I'd made up to play there had been just for me. That's what I'd do again. I didn't need Jon or Amy. I didn't need anyone. I could have fun by myself.

Deciding what to do made me feel better. Now I had other things to think about. Like what I would play on the landing tomorrow. And what the good smell was that was coming from the kitchen.

Casseroles smell better than they taste.

I separated the chicken from the noodles on my plate and tried to decide which to eat first. I like them both, but not together. I couldn't help feeling that Daddy was lucky he had to work tonight — he didn't like casseroles either.

"Maybe I should just print the words." Mama was still thinking about the flash cards.

A picture of what they would look like if Mama printed them went through my head, and I giggled. Mama's printing is awful. The letters lean every which way.

"Don't laugh, young lady!" Mama grinned ruefully. "I know how bad my printing is. But I have to do *something*. Mrs. Strand needs the flash cards tomorrow morning."

I could tell Mama was really worried. I tried to think of some way to help her. That's when I remembered my printing set. It had been so long since I'd used it that I'd almost forgotten that I had it.

Mama's face brightened. "That should do it nicely," she said.

It took me a while to find the printing set. It was under a bunch of stuff on the floor of my closet. When I brought it into the kitchen, I saw that Mama had cleared the table and propped up the list of words for the flash cards against the sugar bowl.

"I only need capital letters," Mama said as I opened the box.

While Mama printed *WITCH* and *GHOST* and the other words on flash cards, I took a sheet of notebook paper and printed my name:

lila ann rocklin

Even without capital letters, I liked the way it looked.

I printed our address. And some of my favorite words. I wasn't sure I'd spelled *lavender* right, but it looked good anyway.

"This is really fun," I said, surprised that it was. I didn't remember thinking so the last time I'd played with it.

Mama looked up and smiled. "Printing sets are fun," she agreed. "I had one when I was your age. I printed menus and valentines and all sorts of things." She laughed, remembering. "Once my friends and I printed a neighborhood newspaper."

A newspaper!

That's what I'd do on the landing tomorrow. I closed my eyes and saw myself writing fast to make the deadline — just like the reporters on television shows did.

Then I saw something else. Jon and Amy coming up to the landing. My stomach tightened. I didn't want to think about them.

I opened my eyes. Making a newspaper by myself was going to be fun. It *was*.

By the time I went to bed, I was almost sure of it.

chapter
·8·

Twenty.

That's how many pieces of paper I'd already squished up. They covered the printing set sitting, unopened, on the table. At the rate I was going, I'd use up a whole tree in one afternoon.

I sighed and leaned back in the chair. A newspaper was a good idea, but figuring out what to put in it was harder than I had thought it would be.

The downstairs door opened, and I heard Amy's voice.

"Jon, do you think Lila put on her play after we left yesterday?"

"Probably."

I heard Amy sigh.

My heart began to beat very fast. I could hear its thump-thump, thump-thump in my ears. In another minute they'd be on the landing. I picked up my pencil and bent my head over the pad of lined paper.

Amy got to the landing first.

"Are you writing another play, Lila?" She sounded hopeful.

"No." I didn't look up. "The landing isn't a stage today."

"Is it a library again?" Jon asked.

I shook my head.

"Well, then, what are you doing?"

I drew a lightning bolt on the paper. "I'm being a reporter. The landing is a newspaper office."

"A newspaper office! That sounds like fun!"

"Can we be reporters with you?" Amy asked.

I didn't have to think about what to say. I'd decided. "I don't need other reporters. I can do my newspaper myself."

There! It was done. My heart was still thumping, but I sat calmly, waiting for them to go back down the stairs.

They didn't go.

"I know you *can*," Jon said. "But we'd like to do it with you."

"We really want to, Lila," Amy added.

"You *said* you wanted to be in my play too." I hadn't meant to say that. The words just spit themselves out.

A pained look crossed Jon's face. "Yes, and I wish we had! It would have been more fun."

Amy nodded in agreement. "Alan gave us each one turn on his new bike — from my building to Jon's and back again. Then he said we couldn't ride anymore; his dad wouldn't like it." She looked down and smoothed out her skirt. "I wanted to come back up to the landing, but I wasn't sure you'd want me to."

I didn't say anything — there wasn't anything to say.

"Come on, Lila," Jon urged. "Let us be on your newspaper with you. It'll be more fun if we all do it."

I had just learned something. When you figure out something that you're going to say, you should also figure out what the other person will say back. I hadn't done that. So I was back where I started. Having to decide what to do.

I drew another lightning bolt on the paper.

Part of me wanted to do my newspaper myself. It was safer. But the other part of me knew that Jon was right. It *would* be more fun if we all did it together.

I sighed. "All right. You can be reporters too."

Amy grinned.

"What do we do first?" Jon asked.

"Think of something that's news to write about. Then we'll print it." I pushed the squished-up papers off the printing set and showed it to them.

Amy picked up one of the pieces of paper and smoothed it out. "The first grade at Clinton School has some new flash cards," she read aloud.

"That's not *news*," Jon said.

I knew that. That's why I'd squished it up.

"What is news, anyway?" Amy asked.

Questions are easy. It's answers that are hard. And I hadn't figured out the answer to that one. Although . . .

"The weather report."

Jon and Amy looked at me as if I'd said something in gibberish.

"*That's* not news," Jon said flatly.

"I know," I said, trying to keep the idea that had just floated into my head from floating out again. "That's just it. There's other things in a newspaper besides news."

It was a minute before either of them looked anything but blank.

Then Amy said, "Recipes. My mother cuts them out and tapes them on the refrigerator."

I nodded.

It took Jon longer to understand. Then his face lit up. "You mean things like my dad reads out loud at breakfast. About books. Or movies."

It's nice to be understood. "That's right. I thought that since we weren't exactly sure what news was . . ."

Jon didn't let me finish. "Comic strips! Those are in newspapers too." He grinned. "That's what I'll put in ours. I'll call it 'The Adventures of Ant Man.' " He picked up the pad of paper and tore off a few sheets.

I shuddered. Ants! Jon and his bugs!

"Give me some of that paper, Jon," Amy said, taking

a pencil out of the pickle jar. "I've thought of what I'll write about. Lila's play. Then whoever reads our newspaper will want to see it. We can put it on for a real audience." She sprawled on the floor of the landing.

Jon drew for a minute. Then he looked up. "What are you going to put in the newspaper, Lila?"

I didn't have to think. The smell that had drifted down from the third floor had told me. "A cookie recipe. Mrs. Sweeney is baking today. She'll give me a recipe."

I had started up the stairs when I heard the downstairs door open.

"Amy? Jon? Are you up there?" It was Alan.

"Yes," Jon called back. "We're here."

"Go get your skates and let's race."

My hand tightened on the banister. It was going to be just like yesterday. Amy and Jon would go. . . . I took a deep breath. I wasn't going to *let* it be like yesterday. I wasn't going to wait for Alan to be mean to me again.

"Go ahead, Jon," I said loudly. "And you too, Amy. I'd rather do my newspaper by myself anyway."

Then I ran the rest of the way up to the third floor.

chapter
·9·

I looked over the railing.

The landing was empty, just as I'd known it would be. I closed Mrs. Sweeney's door and went down the stairs, stopping on my way to pick up Jon's comic strip.

Alan's wanting to have a skate race was a way to keep Jon and Amy from playing with me. I was sure of it, but I still didn't know why.

"I don't care." I said the words as loud as I could. Maybe that would make them true.

It didn't.

But even if I did care, I wasn't going to let Alan spoil what I played on the landing. Not today. I'd do my newspaper anyway. I'd write all the things for it myself. And it would be terrific. I'd even thought of a name for it:

The Landing Flash

It looked good written in red pencil. It would look even better in print. I leaned back in my chair, feeling pleased with myself.

"Well, if you don't want to skate and you don't want to ride my bike, what *do* you want to do?" Alan's voice echoed up the stairwell.

"Play up on Lila's landing," Amy and Jon answered at the same time.

The pencil fell out of my hand. They hadn't gone!

"What do you want to do that for? What's so good about her landing anyway?"

"It's not the landing," Jon said. "It's the things that Lila thinks up to do on it."

"Like that dumb play yesterday?"

"It wasn't a dumb play!" Amy sounded just as angry as Alan did.

"I don't know why you bother with Lila at all," Alan said. "She's no fun to be with."

"That's not true," Jon said.

"No, it isn't," Amy agreed. "The things she thinks up are lots of fun to do!'"

My breath caught in my throat. I couldn't believe what I was hearing. Jon and Amy were *arguing* with Alan — and sticking up for me!

"Come on up, Alan," Amy said. "You'll see what fun it is."

"No, I won't," Alan said angrily. "Because I'm not

going up there. *I'm* going skating."

The downstairs door slammed.

"Did Mrs. Sweeney give you the recipe, Lila?" Amy asked as she got to the landing.

I was too surprised by what I'd heard to say anything. I just nodded.

"Good," Jon said. Then he looked to where he'd been sitting on the stairs. "What happened to my comic strip?"

"It's here," I said. "I picked it up. I thought . . ." There wasn't any need to say what I'd been thinking. It hadn't happened.

Jon didn't seem to notice. "So far I have Ant Man lifting a car. Maybe I should have him lift a building too." He took the sheet of paper I held out and sat back down on the stairs. "No, I'll save that for another time when we do a newspaper." He bent over the paper.

Jon was drawing. Amy, sprawled on the floor of the landing, was writing. I was the only one not doing anything. I couldn't. I was still too surprised that they were there.

A few minutes later, just as I'd picked up my pencil and begun to write again, the downstairs door opened and Alan came up the stairs.

"It's no fun skating by myself," he said glumly.

Without looking at me, he stepped over Amy and

crossed the landing to where Jon was sitting. "What are you doing up here anyway?"

"We're being reporters on Lila's newspaper," Jon said without looking up.

"Newspaper! Reporters! *That's* fun?"

Jon went on drawing. "We think it is."

"More fun than skating or riding bikes?" It was clear that Alan didn't believe him.

"Lots more fun," Amy said.

"But what about *me?*"

"What about you?" Jon said. "You didn't want to do what we wanted to do. You said so."

The sudden blotch of red on the back of Alan's neck told me that he didn't like having his words tossed back at him.

"Maybe I'll change my mind," he said belligerently.

Jon looked up. "If you want to be a reporter too, Alan, you'll have to ask Lila. It's her newspaper."

Alan's shoulders stiffened, and the red blotch spread up to his ears. He didn't turn around. And he didn't say a word.

Suddenly I knew that he didn't want to ask me. Anything.

I wondered how long he would just stand there.

Then Amy giggled. "Alan, you're acting as if you think Lila's going to bite you."

Alan spun around and glared at her. "Don't be dumb," he snapped.

"*I'm* not the one who's being dumb," Amy retorted.

"She's right, Alan," Jon said.

I watched the color drain out of Alan's face. He looked uncertainly from Amy to Jon. And his mouth began to quiver.

"I know how to find out things," he muttered. "I'd be a good reporter."

"You probably would," Jon agreed. "But it's not up to me. It's up to Lila."

My heart began to thump. Now was my chance to get back at Alan for all the times he'd been mean to me. I could say, "No, Alan, *we'll* be reporters. You can just watch."

It would serve him right. That's what he'd done to me.

chapter
·10·

$\mathbf{M}$y chair creaked.

It was the only sound on the landing. Nobody was moving. Nobody was even breathing. I had the feeling that any minute somebody was going to pop.

Probably Alan.

His fists were clenched, and his neck was stretched as far up as it could go. If he'd stood any stiller, he'd have turned into a statue. The only part of him that was moving was his lips. They were quivering again.

He looked scared.

I had to be imagining it. What could Alan be scared *of*? That I wouldn't let him play newspaper with us? So what if I didn't? He'd just go do something else.

Or would he? Something that he'd said to Jon pinged in my head. And I knew that I wasn't imagining anything. If I didn't let Alan play with us, he wouldn't do something else. He couldn't. He needed other people to do things with.

Alan was scared to be by himself.

Maybe, I thought suddenly, that was the trouble all along. Maybe Alan thought that if Amy and Jon liked being with me, they wouldn't want to be with him. It would explain why he'd tried to keep them from playing with me.

I didn't know that it was possible to feel sorry for someone who'd been as mean to me as Alan had. But I did.

"It's all right, Alan," I said. "You can be on my newspaper."

A weak smile of relief replaced the quiver on his lips, and he nodded.

Jon sighed. "Good, that's settled," he said. And he went back to drawing his comic strip.

Alan sat down on the stairs and watched him.

"Don't just sit there, Alan," Amy said. "Think of something to write about for the newspaper."

"I *am* thinking," Alan said. "In fact, I've just thought of a great idea. I'll write about a skate race that we'll have on Saturday."

Jon looked up. "Who would be the racers?"

"We would, of course," Alan said.

"Lila too?" Jon asked.

Alan flushed. Then he looked at me. "You're a terrible skater," he said.

From the limp way he said it, I knew that my being

clumsy didn't really matter. That it probably never had. He'd used it as an excuse.

Besides, he was right.

I nodded. "Yes, I guess I am."

"That doesn't matter," Jon said.

"The more you skate, the better you get," Amy pointed out. "Lila just needs to skate a lot."

It made me feel good to hear Jon and Amy sticking up for me again, although I didn't think they really needed to. I had a feeling that Alan was through leaving me out of games.

"All right," Alan agreed quickly. "Lila too."

Jon smiled.

"I have an idea," I said. "How about having a prize for the winner of the race?"

"I'll vote for that!" Amy said.

Alan grinned and started to write.

Amy finished writing first. "I'm ready to start printing," she announced.

"Set up the letters," I said, pushing the printing set toward her.

"Wait a minute,"Alan protested. "We have to figure out what goes where on the page. She can't print until we're all finished."

That made sense.

"Now this is the way we'll print it," Alan said when the rest of us were finished. "Amy's story up here, Lila's recipe underneath it. Jon, your comic strip will go on this side and my story below that."

I almost laughed out loud.

Alan can no more help being bossy, I guess, than I can stop making up stories and plays and games.

"This is terrific!" Alan said later, as we were admiring the first finished copy of our newspaper.

"We told you Lila thinks of fun things to do," Amy said. Then she giggled. "Alan, you have measles. Black ones."

She had spots of ink on her face and arms, too. We all did. There were even some spots on our clothes. I was glad I'd decided that reporters wore old comfortable jeans and sweatshirts.

Alan spit on his fingers and tried to wash away the ink measles on his arm. "What's the landing going to be next?" he asked without looking up.

Before I could say anything Jon said, "Come up and see, Alan. That's what I'm going to do."

"Me too," Amy said.

Alan raised his head and looked all around the landing. Then he looked at me. "Maybe I'll do that," he said. "Maybe I will."

Then he smiled, and the ink smear on his upper lip went up at each end. It looked just like a magician's mustache.

And that gave me an idea.

It would be fun to have a magic show on the landing. I wondered if Alan knew any magic tricks.

Well, I'd find out — tomorrow.

A Note to the Reader

Writers are often asked how much of a story is really true. While it's true that when I was Lila's age I made up stories and plays and things to do on the landing of my apartment building, the truest parts of this story are Lila's feelings. They are very much like those I had at her age. And the truer the feelings are in a story, the harder it is to write. So the writing of this story was very hard for me. Many times during the two and one-half years that it took me, I wanted to give up. But because of my editor — a man named James Giblin (whom I call Jim) — I didn't.

Editors' names are not usually found in books because most editors believe that what they do should remain "behind the scenes" and not get in the way between the writer and the reader. It is a kind of unwritten "rule."

I broke that "rule" because I wanted you to know that without Jim Giblin's unwavering belief that Lila's story was worth telling, I could never have written it and looked forward to your reading it.